ALSO BY CATHERINE BUSH

Minus Time